Jake
and the Babysitter

Jake's bear

This Jake book
belongs to

. . . .

To Clare and Daniel and our adventures
—with love

First published 1991 by Macmillan Children's Books, an imprint of Macmillan Publishers Limited.

First U.S. edition 2002

Library of Congress Cataloging-in-Publication Data

James, Simon, date.
Jake and the babysitter / Simon James. — 1st U.S. ed.
p. cm.
Summary: Because only someone who does not know Jake would babysit him, his parents call the new neighbor, and Jake has a surprising evening.
ISBN 0-7636-1800-4
[1. Babysitters—Fiction. 2. Behavior—Fiction. 3. Gorilla—Fiction.] I. Title.
PZ7.J1544 Jat 2002
[E]—dc21 2001058259

10 9 8 7 6 5 4 3 2 1

Printed in Hong Kong

This book was typeset in Usherwood Book.
The illustrations were done in watercolor and ink.

Candlewick Press
2067 Massachusetts Avenue
Cambridge, Massachusetts 02140

visit us at www.candlewick.com

Jake and the Babysitter

Simon James

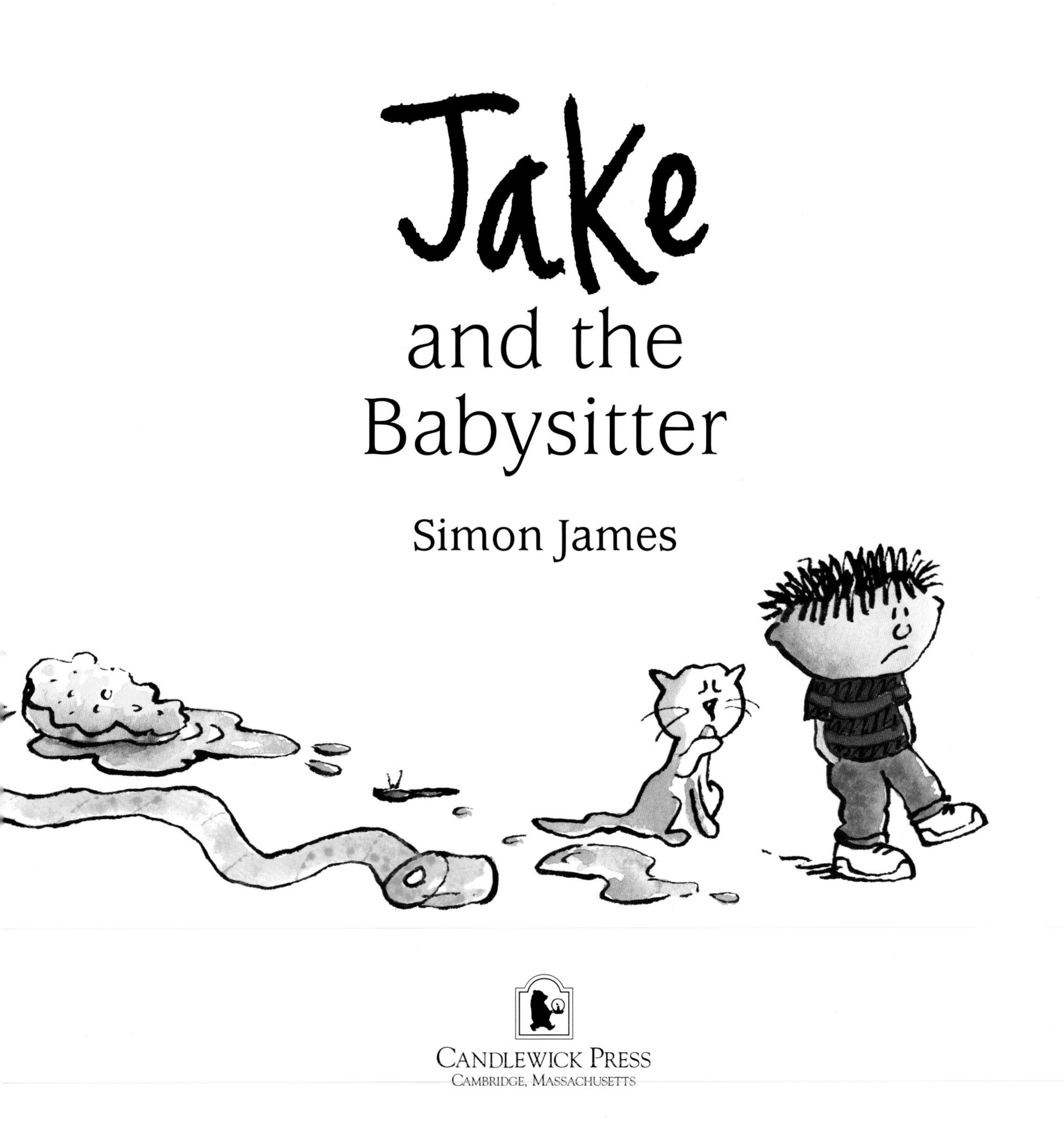

CANDLEWICK PRESS
CAMBRIDGE, MASSACHUSETTS

Jake was difficult.
Jake was a problem.
No one who knew Jake would dare to babysit him.
So his father had phoned the new neighbor.

Jake's
secret stolen
cookie box

Jake's parents were worried.
His mother sighed. "Perhaps he's changed his mind."
But at last there was a knock on the door.
"You must be our new neighbor," said Jake's father. "It's so nice of you to come."

Upstairs, Jake and Timmy the cat prepared for battle.
Once Jake's parents had left, they sneaked
down to watch the late movie.
But after a while, the babysitter started making
strange sniffing noises, as if he could smell
someone in the room.

Suddenly a huge hairy hand pulled Jake out
from under the sofa.
This couldn't be the new neighbor.
It was the most enormous babysitter
Jake had ever seen.
Jake tried to smile . . .

and the babysitter smiled back.
For a moment Jake thought the
babysitter might eat him, so he
quickly pointed to the kitchen.

The babysitter was very hungry. Together
they ate Frozen Fish Fingers, alphabet
soup, and ice cream.
Afterward they both burped out loud.
"What a nice babysitter," thought Jake,
who decided to show him his bedroom.

Jake, Timmy, and the babysitter crept upstairs past Jake's sister's bedroom. Then they bounced up and down on Jake's bed—until the legs broke.

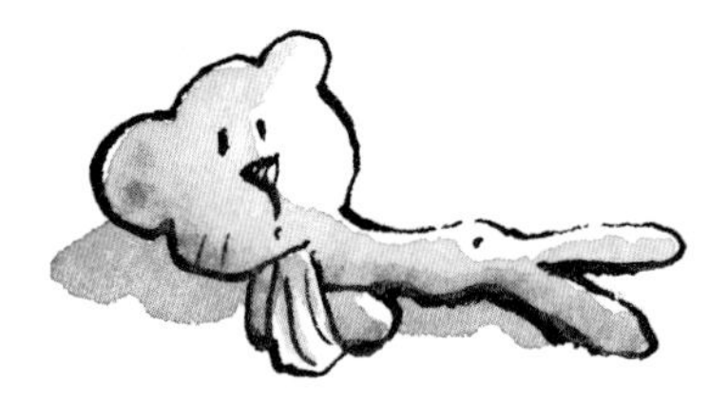

They slid back down the banister to
the living room . . .

where they danced to old Elvis Parsley records that belonged to Jake's dad. Finally, they sat down to watch a really scary horror movie.

It was nearly midnight and time for Jake's parents to come home. How could Jake explain what had happened to the house?

Perhaps it was time for bed, he thought. So he said good night to the babysitter.

When Jake's parents got home they couldn't believe their eyes. How could the babysitter have made such a terrible mess?
They refused to pay him and ordered him to leave immediately.
But the babysitter didn't really mind.

And the next day neither did Jake.
He knew he'd had the best babysitter — ever!

Love from the Babysitter

SIMON JAMES is the author-illustrator of many acclaimed books for children, including *The Day Jake Vacuumed, Jake and the Babysitter, Jake and His Cousin Sidney, Days Like This, The Wild Woods*, and *Leon and Bob*, which was named a New York Times Book Review Best Illustrated Children's Book of the Year.